An Echo from the Stars

copyright 2021 Ron Rundle

all rights reserved

published by Fiesta Creative Arts

printed by Kindle Direct Publishing

a division of Amazon

ISBN: 9798490623052

to order visit amazon.com

Barnes and Noble or contact me

Text, layout, editing and cover art by

Ron Rundle

ronrundle@gmail.com

https://fiestacreativearts.godaddysites.com/

All Titles by R. Rundle

Suggested Grades

Miss Angela (gr. 4 - 6)

The Walker Boys (gr. 4 - 6)

The Dark Side of the Moon (gr. 7 & up)

*Adventures in Babysitting (gr. 5 - 8)

*Adventures in Babysitting: I Have a Dark Passenger (gr. 6 - 8)

Marginal Waters: Monster's Edition (gr. 6 - 8)

This is New (gr. 7 - 10)

Just an Ordinary Joe (gr. 8 - 10)

Pearl (gr. 8 & up)

Rocket Girl (gr. 8 - 10)

There's a New Girl in Town (gr. 7 - 10)

Dragon (gr. 6 - 10)

**The Brat Chronicles (gr. 6 - 8)

**Wherever I Go (gr. 8 & up)

**The Vagabond Gene (gr. 8 & up)

**The Vagabond Princess (gr. 8 & up)

A Passing Ship (gr. 7 & up)

Ride (gr. 8 & up)

An Echo from the Stars (gr. 8 & up)

Living in a Land of Make Believe (gr.8 & up)

High School

Starfinder

High School & Adult

***Marginal Waters

***Marginal Waters: The After Party

***Marginal Waters: The Invasion of the Woodpeckers

***Marginal Waters: I Have a Dark Passenger

***Marginal Waters: The Brat Chronicles

Rumble Doll

Melancholy With No Obvious Cause

Days of Future Past

Sequential Titles   * ** *

Who am I?

Dave and his long time buddy sat on a low bridge spanning the little creek they fished in on Saturday mornings. It was not Saturday morning but late Saturday evening, didn't matter, it was their hang out place light or dark. They had finished farm chores and were just hanging out before Joey would have to go home.

Dave was looking up at the sky; he found lately he was doing that a lot, but not sure why. To say Dave had been feeling distracted and downright odd for a while was an understatement. But in typical male fashion he was keeping his feelings to himself rather than sharing them with anyone. But Joey was his absolute best bud and wingman, who else would he talk to. The longer he thought about it the more he figured maybe it was time.

Now many adults would say, what about his parents. He had thought about that but his mom was very protective and any minor issue in Dave's life in the past became a major crisis for her. In short, he really didn't want to upset her. His dad was not currently living with them, so, tough to consult on any subject. But he figured, at some point, he had to come out with it.

"Joey, ever wonder who you are?" This was fairly clear cut for his buddy.

"I'm Joey or Joseph as my mom always calls me when she's ticked." That wasn't what Dave meant.

"No, ever think there could be somebody else in part of your brain?" Joey was no help.

"My sister's in my brain, gives me a headache, she's a pain in the butt, head, and everywhere else." Dave did not share Joey's feeling about his sister.

"She's alright." Joey made kissing sounds.

"That's 'cause you like her." Dave gave him a shove.

"Do not." Shove back from buddy.

"Do."

"Do not, well, maybe just a bit." Joey had what he thought was a great solution.

"You see, I notice things, you want her, get your mom to adopt her." Dave just gave him a look. "Yeah, guess that wouldn't work, well it would for me, but...." Joey's brain tended to wander off the topic quite easily. As usual Dave steered him back on track.

"Could we get back to my question?" Joey had forgotten.

"What was your question?" Dave rolled his eyes.

"You've taken too many foul tips. The question was ever feel there's someone else in your head? Maybe you have a back story you didn't know about?" His buddy considered those points within his available parameters of reasoning and said,

"Nope." He then lay back on the bridge and looked at the black sky full of stars, he was thinking with an adolescent moment of personal growth, but wandering off the track again said,

"Think there's somebody out there?" That amazingly was the thing that was on Dave's mind. He leaned back next to him, both with hands behind their heads staring up and the black backdrop behind a star lit sky.

"Yes I do." The two of them were now on their backs, both staring at the same sky millions have people have looked at for as long as we have been here. People had thought about the same thing they were thinking right now. Are we it? Is this planet and the disorganised, occasionally violent mass of people on it, it, nothing else? Finally Joey got his head back on his buddy's problem.

"Who's in your head with you?" Dave, though he felt the problem had no ideas.

"I don't know; I just feel like something's wrong." He tapped his head. "Like somebody else is in there." He pointed at the sky. "Maybe I have a long lost brother out there somewhere." Joey had a point.

"So he'd be out there, not in your head." Dave thought,

"Maybe both." Now that got Joey's attention.

"Whoa, you losing it?" That had crossed Dave mind.

"Maybe, hope not." He pulled something out of his pocket. "And then there's this."

This was a cylindrical object and ten centimetres long and maybe two centimetres wide, rounded at both ends. Joey looked,

"What is it?" Dave shook his head,

"Not a clue."

"Can I?" Dave handed it to him.

"Don't drop it." Joey cradled it in his hands.

"All right, all right." He rolled it around in his hands.

"Where'd you get it?" At this point Dave knew this story was like a hand grenade with the pin still in it. Pull the pin and who knows what.

"Give it back." Joey did. Dave held it in his hand and made the call.

"I pooped it out." At that point they could hear Joey laughing up at the house.

"Right, Dave, really, really, me too many foul tips?" He cupped his hand near Dave's ear and said, "anybody home?" He looked in Dave's right ear. "Wait, I see daylight out the other side. How about tin foil in your hat?" Now Dave got serious.

"You think I could make that up? I'm telling you that's what happened." Joey was trying to follow the story.

"So, you must have ate it." Dave shook his head.

"How, can't chew it, can't swallow it whole, that's a heck of a big pill." Joey looked at it closer.

"Did it hurt?" Dave laughed,

"Not really but I heard it clink." Joey burst out laughing again, thinking, not the sound you expect to hear when at work on the pot.

"How you get it out?" Dave shrugged,

"My aquarium net. It's in the dump now." Joey waved his hand so Dave would hand it back. He went to take took it back, but stopped.

"It been cleaned?" Dave laughed,

"About thirty times."

"What the heck is it, got no switch, nothing, how did it…? Dave.

"I don't know, must have been in there somewhere, somehow. Don't know how it got here, or, what it is." Joey was holding it in two fingers, judging by the size, might smart a bit.

"Didn't you feel it?" Dave laughed at that one.

"On the way out, heck yeah." Joey's imagination wandered.

"Maybe it was planted by the secret service."

Dave laughed,

"I think I would have felt that." Joey nodded.

"Fair point." Dave put it back in his pocket and they both lay back on the old wooden bridge, getting too tired for solving a mystery that deep. Joey offered his last question.

"What you going to do?" Dave,

"No idea,' he looked up. noticing the headlight beams in their driveway. "Your dad's here to get you." Joey gave his buddy a little punch.

"Later bud." He jumped up, "serious, get your mom to adopt Becka, maybe have a spring wedding." Joey laughed. "I know you'd be very happy." Dave just yelled at him,

"Get lost!" Joey disappeared up the hill.

"Later bud."

With that Dave lay back on the bridge and looked at the stars on his own. He pulled the mystery object out of his pocket and looked at it again.

"What the heck are you? How the heck did you get inside me?" Then it vibrated in his hand. "What the…"

After the 'thing', whatever it was vibrated in his hand he figured he had to tell his mom. Maybe Joey was right, could have been planted, maybe a miniature bomb or something. This was getting serious, as he was really starting to think he was losing it, both physically and mentally. Dinner was always late because of her work and his farm chores.

As usual she made enough food to feed a small third world country, David as she always called him never went hungry. All through dinner he was going over in his head how he was going to broach this, still reluctant to upset his mother in any way, lately that appeared to be his dad's job.

He had been picking at his dinner and a teenage boy not interested in eating got noticed immediately.

"David, you ok?"

"Mom, something's going on." His mom dropped her fork and put her forehead on her hands on the table. She sat up and took a moment, but already knew part of the answer.

"Ok, what's going on?" Dave immediately went into mom, I'm ok mode."

"I'm ok, just, been feeling like there's someone else in my head, like a dream that stays in the daytime." He pulled out his new souvenir for lack of a better word. "And there's this, I call it the silver bullet. Mom believe it or not I pooped this out." His mom looked at it and just nodded.

"I knew this would happen." That was not at all what Dave expected to hear and was not amused.

"What, and you didn't tell me!"

"David, I knew it would happen, just didn't know when." He went to argue.

"Mom!"

"Listen, long back story here; your birth was very difficult and really under normal circumstances you wouldn't be here at all. I know you're upset with me. I know the symptoms that go with that thing, but, you're here. You wouldn't be without a lot of stuff even I don't understand. But, you really have to talk to your Grandfather. He can explain all this better than me.

"Gramps, he's grouchy!" His loving daughter knew her dad well.

"Just let a few whiskey's settling in his stomach. Remember I named you after him."

David Joseph or Gramps

Dave stood nervously at his door; it had been awhile since his last visit as Gramps didn't really encourage drop ins. As far as Dave was concerned, he didn't encourage any kind of contact at all. When visiting he would eat and then sit in a corner, not really involved in whatever conversation was going on. And in a Jewish household, family gatherings generally include a lot of conversation. He would slip a small silver flask out of this pocket and sip the contents every once in a while. He seemed to think no one noticed.

He was what you could call an unusual man. Personally, as mentioned, sometimes a little crispy around the edges. Physically you could say he was no oil painting. Getting a little long in the tooth to the point where personal grooming was not much of a priority. He wandered around in old track pants and a tatty sweat shirt. Looking at him you would think, just another unkept geezer, not doing much, probably never did. That would be a huge mistake. I have found that is often true, people are seldom what they seem, often less or more.

He visited Dave and his daughter occasionally but for the most part, kept to himself. There was no grandmother, as he never married. You should be wondering where did Dave's mom come from. Well, another Gramps mystery as he came back from his last tour in Iraq with his service revolver and a baby. It was assumed but never confirmed that daughter was the product of an affair, or perhaps just an adult relationship that reached its end game. Questions were never encouraged, as that generation of men seldom talked about their personal lives. But Dave's mom was named Cala, which is a name with definite Arabic influences. It means castle or stronghold in Arabic. Cala the daughter had very olive skin and dark brown eyes, another clue as to her background. There was continuous irony in Gramps life as he was definitely Jewish in background, yet Cala's mom had to be Arabic. Both races of people have a fairly long history of not getting along at all. At some point somebody must have got along, because Cala was born. There was much more.

Gramp's own parents, now long gone had migrated from Israel to Canada after living through several wars with their Arabic neighbours. Their house had been destroyed twice by SCUD missiles, just bad luck as the missiles were not really guided. Once they were over the target area they just ran out of fuel and fell from the sky. Fortunately, they were at work both times or our story would have ended there.

You could say that Gramps had definitely been around. He got passed over for jobs in his field in data retrieval and computer programming. He started his adult working life in the U.S. military as a jarhead. That is a nickname for a field soldier. That is pretty common in the U.S. with lots of poor black and white kids with limited job opportunities. Since the U.S. was heavily involved in Iraq, Gramps figured he'd take a a few chunks out of several Arabic soldiers as payback for the SCUD missiles on his parents.

He found that revenge was not very rewarding. He did three tours in Iraq and realised quite early on he was fighting a war that no one could win. He managed to survive what his brother in arms called 'the big suck'. He came home not so messed up he couldn't function and managed to avoid getting any limbs blown off.

He found that the instilled hatred he had for all Arabic people was misplaced. He learned the Iraqis had fought the

Russians, the U.S. and United Nations forces. They did this while dealing with internal tribal conflicts; the Taliban, then I.S.S.I.S. This was done while trying to stay alive and raise families. He found they were much tougher than any of their enemies believed. The more you wailed on them, the tougher they got. Once you got clear of the political animals in the culture, the rest were just people, perhaps a little different from him but that's all. They were just trying to survive in a very harsh and hostile environment.

Then there was one girl in particular he met during a raid, she crawled out from under her dead parents who had shielded her from a hail of gunfire. That was the final piece of evidence that proved they were like most parents, just trying to protect their child. As he helped this terrified and despondent young woman get out of the rubble he said to himself,

"I can't do this anymore." He became relentlessly protective of this orphaned girl and eventually they became a couple. His plan was to return to the U.S. with his new child and wife but she was killed by the Taliban after their baby was born. Her crime was consorting with the enemy. His sadness was so enormous, he thought about joining his girl wherever she was. But who would look after their baby? With nothing left to stay for and his tour over, he came home, as mentioned, with a pistol and baby Cala. He knew the only way he would use the pistol again was if someone were trying to hurt his daughter.

Though his soldiering days were over the U.S. military finally realised he had special skills in data mining and transfer, and also genetic research. They decided he was useful and hired him into the Pentagon. From there his personal life ended as his Iraqi sweetheart was remembered fondly and never replaced. His daughter Cala would be the only woman in his life. He was her father and forever guardian angel.

Now along the way to being not too messed up he like most soldiers in Iraq dabbled with varies pills, powders and potions to the point where he knew from his scientific background there would likely be some genetic damage that would be passed on to his only child. That would also be passed on to any children she had. So when his daughter excitedly told her dad that her and her husband were thinking about starting a family he had to say,

"There could be complications with that." This is not what daughter one and only wanted to hear. However, he had a solution.

"Let me do a DNA scan and see if everything is ok." Her only question was,

"And if it ain't?" Her dad said,

"There is an external fix." This he knew was problematic depending on how serious the damage was and how generous and knowledgeable colleagues would be. She had no idea what the external fix was or just how complicated it was, but it sounded like what she wanted to hear. Soon David was born, named after Cala's protective father. His daughter had a good sense that her beloved son would not have been born without her father's help.

The Echo Has Found a Home

Gramps welcomed his grandson to his home;

"David, you've grown a foot!" Dave smiled,

"Not really Gramps." Gramps was welcoming,

"How 'bout a beer?"

"I'm thirteen Gramps."

"Ah you're so darned tall, hard to keep track. Not good with numbers any more." Dave laughed to himself, knowing Gramps had an advanced degree in mathematics. He paddled down the haul and called back,

Come on in, take a load off." Dave sat down and thought he'd get right to the point and took out the 'silver bullet' and laid it on the table.

"I pooped this out." Gramps picked it up, staring at it in what seemed to Dave as complete admiration. He rolled it around in his hand; he seemed almost in awe.

"You've been getting someone else in your head?" Dave nodded.

"What is it?" Gramps was still holding it in admiration.

"Basically among other things, it's a cosmic antenna." Dave laughed,

"So I can get NHL hockey on it?" Gramps shook his head.

"No, but I'll bet you're getting messages out of what appears to be nowhere."

"Yeah, I see someone walking in a fog; they like, whisper to me." Gramps nodded.

"Girl, boy?" Dave wasn't completely sure.

"Girl I think, not sure; what's going on Gramps?" Gramps got up, slowly. He winced on the way up. He thought he heard the universal expletive come out under his breath.

"Lot's of fun getting old, but I need something from the bar." Dave rolled his eyes as he watched his old grandfather shuffle into the next room. He just wanted the story. The old guy shuffled back and sat down with a grunt. He looked at the amber liquid in his glass with what almost seemed like fondness. He took a sip and smiled, it seemed to help.

"Ok, what you're going through, has happened only once before, most likely will never happen again, but you're going to be ok. Just that, your life is going to get more complicated." Dave was getting some indication of that already.

"How so?"

"Well you're going to have someone else living in there with you." He reached over and tapped Dave on the forehead. Dave being a boy thought about the first thing.

"Is she cute?" His Gramps settled back into big chair and chuckled.

"Sure, why not." Though truthfully, he had no idea who Dave's other personality would be. But there were only two possibilities.

Dave didn't know it but he was sitting on the biggest story, perhaps ever. He suspected something big, but not that big.

"Can I have a sip of that?" Gramps handed him the glass.

"Just a sip." Dave took one and coughed and handed it back.

"That's like drinking fire." Gramps took it.

"Best not to get a taste for that." Then he took a sip himself,

"Ok, this is a big story; I think the biggest there ever will be." He leaned forward, now looking very serious, holding up the pointy finger. "This has to stay in this room, forever. Swear on your family name." Dave nodded.

"Ok, I swear." Gramps smiled, he knew his grandson was honourable.

"Done, good, a man is only as good as his word." He took another sip.

"Firstly my life as a young man had a lot of bad choices." Dave knew a bit.

"You were in the military right?" Gramps nodded, similar to his personal life, he had never shared much of his military background either. Most soldiers who saw combat don't talk about it. He took another sip, Dave was wondering how many he would need.

"All soldiers see things, some horrific, seen people die, comrades, innocent civilians." He took another sip. "There's no glory in war son." He seemed distracted for a minute looking off. Dave figured correctly, remembering.

"All it amounts to is destruction, pain and death. He took another sip and looked off into the distance again. He could see them all like it was yesterday. He shook his head to bring him back into the present.

"But, to cope most of us drank, smoked, took whatever pill or powder we could get to help us through it." Dave smiled,

"Now it's just booze." Gramps gave him a look.

"Never mind the high ground; I still see most of their dead faces; I'm old, alone, and, I don't care anymore. Wait till you get here." He paused and took another sip; David could see he offended him.

"Sorry Gramps." He reached over and gave him a gentle pat; the apology was accepted.

"Anyway I knew my DNA was messed up. Again, then, didn't care, but, along came your mother. I knew it would mess up her's and likely any kids she had. So I found a fix, mostly by accident, but," He paused and took a sip mostly to compose how he was going phrase the next part. Dave said,

"But?"

"But there's was a significant side effect for your mother, and now you. "You have discovered part of it." Now Dave was really concerned.

"Part!" Gramps finished his whiskey, "hold that thought." He got up and shuffled back to the bar, called back on his way, "and don't be rolling your eyes." Dave smiled, he'd already done that. He came back, grunted and sat down, taking a sip.

"Ah, that's better." Ok I discovered what the damaged parts of your DNA were, encapsulated the information and sent it everywhere, call it an SOS, hoping someone, somewhere could help fix this problem. Dave nodded remembering some of his early but not continued Jewish religious education.

"Isn't there something about the sins of the father?" Gramps nodded,

"Well said and true David, the full quote is 'He will by no means clear the guilty, visiting the iniquity of the fathers on the children to the third and the fourth generations.'" Dave shook his head.

"God's a little harsh." Gramps nodded.

"True, Jewish God, not what you'd call forgiving. I think it also means don't look at me to fix the problems you caused. So long story short, I got an answer, an energy transfer, including the DNA fix, from," he took a big sip and pointed up at the sky. Dave's eyes widened.

"From space!" Gramps took another sip and looked up as well.

"I call it an echo from the stars. I sent out a ping, and got an echo back. The first one was for your mother, the second is for you.

"So mom's been through this?" Gramps nodded.

"Still is, so talk to her, ask her what it's like now, she knows all about this. That's why she worries so much about you."

"So what can I expect?" Another sip, "hang on, just going to freshen." Another grunt, he went shuffling down the hall, pointing back at him without turning around, "no eye rolling!" Dave called to him.

"Why don't you just bring the bottle?" Now he stopped and turned, Dave noticed that old people shuffle their turns, taking little steps to complete the one eighty. Gramps said,

"First rule of drinking, never drink with the bottle beside you." Dave laughed,

"I thought the first rule of drinking was don't drink too much." Gramps smiled and pointed.

"You take liberties young man, but I love you anyway." He came back with his glass topped up. Dave noticed Gramp's world view seemed to improve with each refill.

"Ok, you will have their personality with you all the time. You'll know some of what they're thinking; they know some of what you're thinking, call it, cosmic schizophrenia." Dave was getting concerned.

"They don't tell you to gouge your eyes out."

"Not according to your mom; she says they're pretty good company. Dave was truly blown away.

"That's so so weird, why do they do that; why wouldn't they just stay inside their own head?" He looked over and Gramps had nodded off; the whiskey and time had taken its toll. Dave found a blanket and gently spread it over him, found a bottle of water. Dave thought, the last one was a pretty good question, but it looked like the story teller was done for the night. He patted him on shoulder gently and let himself out.

"Goodnight Gramps."

The Echo

"So, sweetheart, how's it going?" He touched his lovely daughters hair. Tahlia giggled and blushed. She had been living in a somewhat intimate way with a thirteen year old earth boy for a few weeks now.

"He's funny, confused, all this is getting to him a bit."

"He'll understand soon." She laughed and added.

"He thinks about girls a lot, but I think he's ok." Tahlia had been given the earthly name as her dad realised she would be one of her planet's two travellers. Her dad had met old David many years ago. A chance encounter across millions of miles of black nothing. The early genetic link to Cala had given Tahlia's dad a glimpse of another world. He wanted his daughter to have the same experience and also was happy to help sustain a successful life to another human, even though far away. Anything alive seems to know instinctively that life is precious.

What he didn't know was that his daughter was not content to explore the universe just to live in the corner of someone's brain. She had seen through young David that the planet Earth was a fertile place, full of the kind of beauty that her home planet simply had forgotten to value.

What was a natural world at one time had been replaced by the end game of inorganic chemistry. That is all food and life sustaining oxygen was generated by various industrial processes. The world was clean, comfortable, but the only green was artificial turf and plants.

This issue came up at one of their family dinners. She had been thinking about nothing else for weeks and finally got enough courage to raise the subject.

"Dad, I want to travel to earth, meet David and his mother." His answer was not unexpected.

"Darling, I don't want you to leave. And it could be very risky." He put his head in his hands.

"And I would likely never see you again." She really did not want to upset him, but the need to wander was so powerful. The other issue was her mother had died doing planetary exploration in a space shuttle, common as mud, but accidents happen.

Now her dad had significant scientific skills himself and connections to other scientists who most likely could give his daughter what she wanted. Also, in this world, all children at thirteen were free to make their own calls. His daughter had decided. Her father was not even close to happy with his daughter's adventurous spirit, and truthfully since his wife died, she was his whole world. Though he did not have a problem with her exploring existentially, leaving the planet was not what he wanted.

This was a most significant decision as her body including all the information her brain had absorbed to date would have to be deconstructed and reduced to a photon. That photon could travel at the speed of light, actually greater due to a particular invention her mother and father had been part of called a photon accelerator. When they did this they did not envision their only daughter being adventurous enough to want to try it out. Once the photon of life got to its destination it would reassemble into a thirteen year old girl. Getting back home would be unlikely, because earth did not have the technology to generate the return trip. If her dad wanted to see her again he would have make the trip himself. Trial runs had been made using people's bodies that had been donated to science. Actually, all bodies on their planet were donated to science. The bodies were successfully deconstructed, 'launched' so to speak, then reassembled successfully. The rub in all that was they were just dead people who started off that way and came back dead. It had not been tried with a living person. The first trial run would be with his only daughter and the last link in a small family. Her dad made his stand,

"I forbid it and the lab is closed to you!"

'Clink!'

For the next few days Dave kept getting hints from his alter ego, flashes of images of someone who was walking towards him. Similar to more normal dreams but he found it tough to remember what the hint was. Another problem was his best bud Joey was constantly asking him questions, but he had to shake him off and lie. He had given his word to his grandfather and that was that.

Also the hints were starting to get stronger. One day he was in his room supposedly doing homework when he swore he heard someone whisper,

"Hi." He spun around.

"What, who said that?" Of course he was alone in his room. But there was nothing else, but that night he was lying in bed, finding sleep was getting harder to start. He had also heard people who are getting unstable start hearing voices.

"Maybe I'm just going nuts." But this time he had a distinct image of someone walking towards him, but so vague it was impossible to know much about who it was. It was like looking at someone through a white bedsheet held in front of them. Also his stomach was starting to ache a bit.

"Great, getting flu or something." But the next morning he heard it,

Clink.

"What?" Sure enough, mixed in with, well, you know was another one. "Ewe, gross, not what I call fishing." But, it had to be retrieved. After many disinfectant baths

"Ok, think I better visit Gramps again."

After school he was standing at Gramps door. When he opened it he held it out in his hand.

"Got another one." Gramps looked down at it; his eyebrows went up.

"Come on in son." This was new even for grandfather and he truly had no idea why his grandson was getting another signal antenna.

"Could I?" He rolled in around. "It's not the same, heavier, bigger I think." Dave had the other one in his pocket and put it in Gramps hand.

"You're right gramps." He looked up. "It was the same size this morning." He was holding them both in his hand.

"Any idea how all this works? How do these things talk to me? What started all this?" Gramps grunted,

"Hold that thought, whiskey." He pointed back as he headed for the bar.

"No comments please." He hustled back, within his ability to hustle.

"Ok, this all started with a message from me. I sent out from my lab by a modified data signal." Dave knew the first part.

"You were asking for help with Mom's DNA?"

"Yeah, sent it everywhere; didn't expect the answer to come from off planet!" Dave asked,

"How was the signal modified?"

"The message is encoded into light beams." To Dave it sounded like science fiction.

"Didn't know we could do that." Gramps took a sip, and sat back looking a little smug.

"Well generally they are sent by fibre optical cables, not just in space. I figured out how to do that, but…whoever is out there is so far ahead of what I did. I can hardly understand it." He glanced at Dave's new cylinder.

"You know it's getting bigger." Dave picked it up, sure enough, it was also a little heavier.

"Could it be dangerous?" Gramps shook his head.

"They've never shown anything like that; the opposite really." He looked at the new cylinder again, "but this is another story."

"What do you think Gramps?"

"They seem to have the ability to compress everything into a photon. That's how I got the DNA fix's for you and your mom got sent to earth. They also have a way to accelerate the speed of photons, don't ask me how they do that. Hold that thought." Dave smiled.

"More whiskey?"

"Just freshen a bit." Up again and down the hall. Dave didn't roll his eyes this time; his Gramps was alright. His mom has filled him in on all the stuff he went through; the things he must have seen. If he wanted to drink whiskey in his old age, what the hey. He returned, you couldn't say in no time and sat down with a plop.

"Ok, your second cylinder." He took a sip and a moment. "I think one of them is coming."

"What!" Gramps nodded.

"That's what I think, you might have a roommate soon." Gramps knew this was completely different. The others are just info and antennas, but this," he held out his hand so Dave would pass it over. He looked at it, with affection. "This is something special; I hope it is another person, I'd love to meet them."

Dude!!

Things continued to spiral for Dave, to where was a question still unanswered. Over the next few weeks Dave's second cylinder continued to grow daily. He became more and more obsessed with it, finding himself sitting and watching it to see if he could actually see it growing. He made up a chart showing circumference and length with the date. The current theory was it was growing about five centimetres a day. He mused,

"How big will it get; maybe there's a monster in there, come to take over the planet. He soon dismissed that theory as his new schizophrenic friend remained a gentle but continuous presence. Though her presence was becoming more pronounced with time. He was now pretty sure it was a girl. She seemed to be commenting on the things he was looking at the way a girl might. But the evidence was still too circumstantial to make the clear call.

It was soon too large for Dave to carry over, so Gramps made a few trips. He would stand over it and put his hand on Dave's back, almost in tears.

"This is so amazing, you know what this means?" Dave shrugged. "We're definitely not alone; and they're a whole lot smarter than us. Dave asked a good question.

"Why are they leaving their planet then?" Gramps gave him a loving look.

"That is a good question son, and I have no answer. Maybe we'll find out." He added,

"All this is still under our hats?" Dave nodded.

"All good Gramps."

But as they say, the times, they are a changing. Dave was eating dinner alone as his mom was working late. He was just finishing when the heard a yell from upstairs.

"Dude! What the friggin heck!" Joey had obviously made his way to Dave's room up the ladder he used from time to time. This was enough to get Dave to bolt up the stairs three at a time. He burst into his room,

"What!" Joey was pointing, but not speaking, finally,

"Look, you, you've, got a...!" Dave noticed immediately the lid was off his growing cylinder. Joey was still pointing,

"Take a look, go on." Dave was hoping there wasn't some kind of alien monster in there. Turns out it wasn't, not at all. He stopped in his tracks, then gingerly peaked inside.

"Whoa!" Joey nodded,

"What'd I say!" Dave looked away.

"Should we be looking?" Joey was not as concerned.

"Heck yeah, man…she's, wow, so, wow!" What they were looking at was a girl, about their age, maybe a little older. The cause for the interest other than it was a girl was she was lying on her back, eyes closed, hands down at her sides, but, completely naked. Apparently interstellar travel does not include clothing. For a couple of thirteen year old boys, this was the definition of a positive new experience. Dave looked again and agreed,

"She is so beautiful." Then he got worried, "is she ok?" Joey was still mesmerised.

"Gotta be!"

"I mean is she alive." Joey just shrugged, still too stunned to do anything. Dave reached in and touched her shoulder.

"She's really warm, must be alive." With that her eyes opened. She just said sleepily,

"Hi David." He leaned in closer, slowly.

"Hi, you're the one who's been talking to me?" She smiled, and nodded, but her eyes looked very heavy.

"Yes, but I'm not ready to wake up yet." She blinked and the top of the cylinder began to close again until there was a little click. The two friends were actually speechless. Finally Joey said,

"How long you been hiding her? And what the heck is this, you been growing girls in your room? That's what I call a science project. Dave still had his mouth open, finally,

"I knew the cylinder was here; knew it was growing, didn't know what was in it. Joey ran his hand over the cylinder.

"You didn't tell me about this." Dave sat down on the bed; the events were starting to add up. He looked at his hands and they were shaking.

"Gramps said don't tell anyone." He grabbed his buddy by the shoulders. "You can't say anything, I mean to nobody!" Joey nodded.

"Ok man, calm down, all good, all good." He kept looking at the cylinder. "So now what? What is she? Were'd she come from? What'd you do, make her? Can I have the kit?" Dave laughed at his hormonal friend.

"Calm down, sit down." Joey sat but kept looking at the cylinder. What was inside would be burned into his brain forever. Dave figured Joey may as well have the whole story.

"You know the cylinder I showed you."

"Yeah."

"Well I...'hatched' another one. This one grew, and grew, until, there she is."

"So you had a baby girl out your butt?" With that even Dave could laugh.

"No dopey, they come as a very small particle, so small you don't feel it hit you, and they grow." Joey finished the thought.

"Inside you, but only so far, then, out they come." Joey added what he thought was a good idea.

"Like an egg." Dave had to agree.

"Yep, I guess, made of some kind of metal, but this one kept growing after I, you know. Didn't know what was inside it, thought it might be some kind of monster alien." Joey laughed at his own comment.

"It was not! Come on, can I have one?" They both looked at the cylinder again, remembering. That was an image they would never forget. Dave agreed.

"I don't think so, not sure how I got this one."

"Your mom know?"

"She knows about the cylinder, not what's in it."

"Well, got to tell your mom, pretty hard to keep her hidden." Joey had an idea,

"I know we can switch, you can have my pain in the butt sister; I'll take," he looked longingly at the cylinder, "whoever the goddess is inside yours." Dave did take a moment to laugh.

"Yeah, your parents won't notice the difference. Bud, this stays right in the room." Joey laughed,

"Everybody would think we're nuts anyway." Joey looked at his watch.

"Guess the lid going to stay closed, got to go home." Dave gave him the pointy finger.

"Joey, remember, nobody knows about this." He laughed and headed for the window.

"Let me know if the lid comes off again." Dave called after him.

"Perv." He just laughed and climbed down the ladder. Dave went over and looked at the cylinder. Looking at it you would have no idea what was inside, but he knew the next character in this part of the story was his mother.

"Nothing to do but wait till she comes home." So he sat at the table eating frozen peas from a freezer bag. It was his favourite snack. He looked up as she hustled in.

"Hello David, what's going on?" Dave thought, there's a question with a big answer.

"Mom, you got to sit down for this one." Of course her immediate concern was for her son.

"Are you hurt or something?" He smiled, good old mom, you got to love her.

"I'm fine mom." He thought, one of Gramp's whiskeys would work right now. Nothing to do but come out with it.

"Mom, you know the cylinder in my room."

"Yes?"

"There's a girl inside it." Surprisingly she just said,

"I figured something like that." Dave just looked. "Remember I've got a guest up here too." She pointed to her head. "I just keep hearing, 'look after her.' Is she ok?"

"Yeah well, she made an appearance in front of Joey." He could see the look of concern on her face. "He's cool." His mother laughed.

"Joey, cool, our Joey, right!" Dave did laugh at that one, remembering his first reaction.

"Well, he'll never be the same but he won't talk about it." His mother looked puzzled.

"Why" Dave blushed.

"She travelled naked." His mom gave him a look.

"So you boys were entertained."

"You know mom, it was, but, she's, I've never seen anything more beautiful in my life." He was remembering now, and the look pleased his mother. "Her eyes are the most amazing mix of green and blue."

"She's alert then?"

"Yeah, but seemed sleepy, said she wasn't ready to wake up then and lowered the lid on the cylinder." Always a mother, now with another child to look after.

"But she's seemed ok?"

"She's ok." She came around and gave him a hug from behind.

"Well, quite a day, son."

"You could say that." It occurred to him that nobody on the planet had ever had a day like that. It also occurred to him that the girl they were looking at was just a kid; and he instantly felt protective of her. His mom yawned.

"I'm hitting the hay got a night shift in twelve hours, you ok?"

"Oh yeah, sleep well." Dave's mother was a nurse so night work and overtime were common. He was about to head off to school and wondered what the girl would do if she decided it was time to wake up. He figured, just check and see if anything was going on. When he got to his room to his amazement the top of her cylinder was up. He tipped toed over to it and looked in. There she was again; he let out an involuntary,

"Oh gosh." Shen she heard him her eyes opened. She smiled and whispered sleepily,

"Hi David." David knelt down put his hands on the side of the cylinder.

"Hi, yourself, you got a name?" She still seemed like she was waking up.

"Tahlia,"

"That's a Jewish name here." She moved just slightly.

"My Dad gave me an Earth name. I think it means dew from heaven." He took another look and thought, you really are from heaven. Then she shivered.

"You ok." She shivered again,

"Cold." Dave rolled his eyes and looked away, thinking, well yeah.

"Be right back." He charged down to the kitchen and found a blanket and put it in the microwave for a couple of minutes. He had seen his mother do that at the hospital where she worked when an older lady said she was cold. He hustled back and spread it over her, and tucked it in a bit.

"There." That helped the other issue in the room as well.

"Oh, thank you, that's so warm." Now that she was covered things actually got a little easier. He crouched down next to the cylinder again. He could hear the school bus honking his horn, but he had other things to think about.

"You feel ok?" She nodded.

"Yes, better, just need a minute before I try to get up."

"Just relax, when you're ready." He spent some time studying her face. Her skin was amazingly fair, not a beach girl. She had really blonde hair, but her eyes were the thing. He was studying them so much she finally said,

"What?" Poor Dave was almost helpless.

"Your eyes are so unusual, and really pretty." She actually blushed a little.

"I think I'm ready to get up, can you help me?" School was long forgotten. Dave thought, yes sir, this is my idea of a science project. She struggled to get up.

"I don't think I can step out of this thing, can you lift me?" Dave thought, ok, never done this before.

"Sure." He helped her sit up put one arm around her back and said, "just lift your knees." He figured this would also be the best way to keep the blanket in place. He picked her up the way he had seen heroes pick up girls in movies.

"Holy mackerel!" She looked up at him, eyes still sleepy.

"What?"

"You don't weight anything at all. How much do you weigh?" She giggled and shrugged.

"No idea, but that's what a girl wants to hear." He sat her up on the edge of his bed. She noticed, he was holding the blanket in place.

"Ok, mom gave me this stuff for you to wear, for now." It was just a top and shorts. "Oh, and this, if you need it." She blushed slightly,

"Don't need it."

"Ok, moving on; I'll look that way and you can get dressed." In no time she giggled.

"All set." Now she looked pretty much like every teenage girl did in the neighbourhood, shorts and a 'T' shirt. But he knew she was truly a special girl, mostly likely the most special girl on the planet. He wondered how much pure human she was. Did she have special powers that could vaporise him he she got mad? Then he looked into her beautiful eyes and thought, she don't look too dangerous to me.

"You hungry?" It seemed to hit her.

"Yes, starving." He got up expecting her to do the same.

"I don't think I can walk yet, can you carry me?" Dave actually laughed; he was getting used to this.

"Heck yeah." He leaned over and picked her up off the bed, amazed again at how little she weighed. He carefully carried her down the stairs. Absolutely can't drop the girl. She kept looking at him amused and she was privately pleased that he was so thoughtful and gentle. On the way down the stairs it hit him.

"You're not inside my head anymore."

"Nope, I'm right here." He looked down.

"Yes you are; I'm glad you're here. She gave him that smile.

"Me too."

"This all must seem really weird to you?" She shook her head.

"Not really."

She actually knew more about life on earth than Dave thought. Because she had been inside his head, she understood the world of the thirteen year old boy quite well. She knew she was pretty, she knew that seeing her naked was quite an event for Dave and his buddy. And because she was actually inside his head knew the thoughts that he kept private. Even his private thoughts were not at all threatening. She decided he was a good guy. With the careful trip downstairs over, he sat her gently down in a chair.

"Ok breakfast, any favourites?" She shrugged,

"You're the chef." Dave thought,

"How about a Davewich?"

"I'm so hungry, whatever."

"Here's some blueberries, you can nibble on those." He started getting organised and looked over; the blueberries were gone. She shrugged. Dave just laughed,

"Peckish?" She actually burst out laughing. Dave decided even her laugh was cute.

"What's peckish mean?"

"Hungry." She repeated.

"Peckish, peckish, that's a fun word; I'll use it. What's that?" Dave had an egg in his hand.

"An egg; they're good but you got to cook them."

"Where they come from?" She was full of questions.

"Chickens." She obviously didn't know everything about Earth.

"What's a chicken." Dave quickly loaded up a U-Tube video on the life of a chicken, thought it might keep her quiet long enough to get her breakfast ready. She watched for a bit, then gasped. Dave noticed.

"What! They poop them out!" Dave laughingly crabbed.

"I'm working life a rented mule over here." She sat up and pretended to zip her mouth closed. Then she got up and moved closer, seemingly fascinated with her breakfast being prepared. She sat with her face resting on her hands near the stove.

"Don't be getting too close, bacon spatters." She went to ask what bacon was but stopped and pretend zipped her mouth closed and moved to the end of the counter. And, she was so hungry she didn't want to slow up the process. He continued to get it ready looked over as she mouthed the word.

"Hungry," then smiled. God thought Dave, she gets more beautiful the more times you look at her. She was still sitting with her lovely face on her hands watching Dave work like a cat impatiently watching its owner get it's food dish ready. Finally he set it down. She grabbed it.

"Baby, come to momma!" You might wonder how Tahlia would come up with such Earth like phrases. Remember she had been living in Dave's head for a while, and obviously had gotten pretty good learning the lingo. Dave started making another one immediately as she seemed to devour the first one. He smiled.

"Still hungry?" She just rolled her finger over while swallowing the last bite, another Earth bound piece of sign language.

"Thirsty too." Dave nodded,

"Of course, you ever had milk?" Her look said no. "Allow me." He poured a glass.

"Never seen this before; where's it come from?" Dave just cued up another video on the life of cows. She got closer and sniffed the milk and took a sip.

"Quite good!"

"Ok, sip your milk and I'll make you another." She sat sipping, mesmerised. Suddenly she burst out laughing, clamping her hand over her mouth. She pointed at the screen.

"They suck it out of their boobs." Dave almost dropped his spatula laughing.

"Well yeah if they don't have a baby. That's where we get it." She looked down at her chest. This planet was full of mysteries she had yet to experience.

"Oh yeah." She put her face back on her hands, looking up, smiling, "Not ready for that yet." Dave nodded somewhat nervously.

"Me either, here." Well after two more of Dave's sandwiches the little girl appeared to finally be full. To Dave's surprise she stretched and said,

"Got to go back to sleep for a while." He was immediately concerned.

"You ok?" She nodded sleepily.

"I was told this would be normal for a few days. Can you carry me back upstairs?" Dave came over and picked her up.

"You're going to be able to walk one day?" Sleepy girl put her head on his chest.

"Oh yeah, not yet though." They got to the bed room.

"The bed ok or do you need the metal thing?"

"The bed's fine." He laid her gently down and pulled a cover over her. Had to admit, he was starting to worry a bit, not sure about what or why. She was asleep pretty much as her head hit the pillow. Dave decided to just sit with her, never bothered with a book or anything, just content to watch her sleep, and to make sure she was ok. He glanced closer from time to time.

"My gosh; she just as beautiful asleep, maybe more." He thought, she sure can eat, but a concern creeped into his brain. Why she needed to sleep after sleeping all night. He laughed to himself, I'm turning into my mother. With that thought he decided he would just sit in his chair and keep an eye on her, not sure why but school was out for today. And truthfully, had nothing more interesting to do. Also, he was a little worried about her even though she said the sleep thing was normal. After a few minutes he realised he had fallen asleep as well and woke up. He looked again, still asleep. He whispered to himself,

"Should I wake her?" He decided, might be a thought, and reached and touched her on the shoulder.

"Tahlia." Nothing; he shook her very gently, nothing. "Ok, now officially worried." He got closer, "Tahlia, come on, wake up." Nothing. "She's warm, but…time to call mom."

"Mom." David never called his mom at work unless it was an emergency.

"David, you ok?" Dave was just this side of complete panic.

"It's Tahlia, we had breakfast and she said she needed a nap, now I can't wake her up."

"She's breathing."

"Yep, slowly."

"David touch her neck see what her heart rate is." Dave did.

"Two, three beats in ten seconds." Now mom was really worried, about a number of things.

"I'll call in 911, stay till they get there and ride down to the hospital on your bike."

"Yeah, ok." She yelled into the phone before he could hang up. "Be careful!" Dave had to laugh to himself, in spite of everything she always had time to worry about him.

"I'll be careful mom." Well he was careful within the bounds of worrying about Tahlia. There were several issues about her that would make her the number one celebrity on the planet. He did not want that.

Bay City ER

Dave's mom was trying to hold things together, but the story was starting to be like a bathtub with too many drains. She was seriously wondering how she was going to keep a lid on things. And she was now taking the view that this little girl was one of her kids and therefore was to be protected unconditionally and worried about endlessly. She started by cornering John Roberts, the attending doctor on call this evening and a long standing professional and personal friend.

"John, I need a favour." He naively figured this was nothing.

"Ok?"

"There's a 911 coming in," she lied, " Dave's cousin."

"Ok?"

"This case has to be unofficial." This of course was absolutely against hospital policy. No one gets treated without the paperwork being done. Her friend wanted details.

"Cala, what's going on?"

"She's got a low heart rate, that's all." She got right in his face. "Just help me out here John, ok, no questions." She pulled back and stood waiting for some kind of answer.

"Have I ever asked for anything?" He had to admit,

"Nope, ok, but, sometimes things get too big to hide you know." The flashing lights broke the conversation.

"Whatever, they're here." With that the ambulance crew were wheeling her in. The little girl looked pale; her eyes were closed. Cala intersected the ambulance crew and directed traffic.

"Hey boys bring her to room three." The ambulance crew knew Cala well, slightly surprised by the room she wanted. "How is she?"

"Stable, really low blood pressure and heart rate, not responsive; that's the worry." Cala wanted to get rid of the ambulance crew as quickly as possible.

"John grab an end and we'll get this girl off the gurney." Unfortunately John grabbed the wrong end, nothing she could do about that now but knew he would notice. "Ok, one, two, three, now." John picked her up by the shoulders and his eyes went really wide.

"What the heck, how much does she weigh?" Cala just shrugged; he was getting nothing, and, this was new to her as well. With the girl in place he started examining her and placed his stethoscope on her chest. He looked at Cala, and put it back in place, looked again.

"Ok, what's going on? Why is this girl's heart in the wrong place?" She put her head down; the merry go round was picking up speed. With that David came running into the room, completely out of breath.

"Is she ok?" Then they heard.

"David." Tahlia's eyes had opened and the first person she saw was not David; she was immediately alarmed. "Who are you?" She looked around. "Where am I?" With that David came running over.

"I'm here, you ok?" Cala came running over as well. She gently brushed some hair off her face.

"Hi kid, we were worried about you, David couldn't wake you up. You're at a local hospital, but not for long." She sniffed a little.

"I'm ok; we sort of hibernate when we're going through this. But I'm fine, can we go home?" Cala said,

"David can you get her in the car: I'll be right out." Tahlia smiled,

"I think I can walk now, but can you just put your arm around me, just in case?" Cala came over.

"Ok dear, let's just sit you up." She sat up, no problems. "You feel ok, not dizzy?"

"I'm fine." David stepped in front of her.

"Ok, I'm going to lift you down, and hang onto you, just in case." She gave him the smile.

"Ok." Cala could see a definite bond growing between her son and this most mysterious girl. He lifted her down, again amazed every time he lifted her at how little she weighed and stood her in front of him, holding her up by the waist. She leaned forward and gave him a little kiss on the corner of the mouth and whispered.

"Thank you for being kind to me." Meanwhile Doctor Roberts was standing back observing a most bizarre real life soap opera unfolding in front of him. Curious by nature and profession he was forming a lengthening list of questions about a number of things. Finally Cala nodded and David got it.

"Come on Tahlia." Doctor Roberts and Cala watched the two of them head down the hall slowly. David's mom noticed she leaned her head against David's shoulder. It was getting more complicated by the minute. His arm gently around her back, hand on waist. David thought, god she feels good, and so warm. Doctor Roberts hadn't noticed that. Her body temperature was in the getting concerned range if she was an earth girl. They got to his mom's little SUV and Dave just lifted her up and sat her in the seat. She commented,

"You're strong."

"You don't weigh anything, why is that?" She shrugged,

"Don't know."

Meanwhile back in the ER things were not quite as romantic.

"Cala, what is going on? What's with that girl?" Dave's mother came to a conclusion.

"Ok, sit and I'll give you a condensed version of the story. He sat down.

"I'm listening."

After about five minutes of backstory, her doctor friend just said,

"Did you just make that up now?" Cala shook her head.

"You think I could come up with that?"

"So it's real." She nodded.

"It's real, you see why this has to stay in house." It wasn't a question.

"I think it's the most amazing story every to have been told on the planet; you have to share it." She actually grabbed him and pushed him against the wall. This was now a mother who had a small idea how her children would be affected. Never mess with a momma lion.

"You need to keep this in house! I'm taking her home, in house, right!" He nodded, but Cala has reservations about how loyal this friend would be.

The Talk

Well Tahlia seemed to have recovered from what appeared to be a catatonic state, but was just some kind of alien hibernation. And of course, she had reconstructed from and photon to what appeared to be a human girl. So some side effects would not be unusual. The fact that all this happened at all was the story. But her trip to the hospital was really not necessary, and now seemed perfectly fine.

The mother in the trio had also noticed her son and her new, well, not sure what to call her were getting along very well. In fact, she was concerned they were getting along a little too well. She was sitting at the table and heard them chatting on the way in from the yard.

"How can someone as cute as you stink at catch?" She noticed that Tahlia giggled and gave Dave a shove.

"Never played catch before; and you stink at throwing." Dave very gently shoved her back.

"I threw you the ball and you ducked." Another friendly shove.

"I didn't know I was supposed to catch it."

"I asked, you want to play catch?" With that she stopped and put her hands on her hips and just said,

"Humpf," and stuck her tongue out at him, spun around, and continued walking. She seemed to have all the little flirty earth girl skills already. Dave just laughed and wondered if girls got taught all that stuff or just came by it naturally.

"Jump up on the seat there I'll get us some lemonade." They had a swing seat that was up and a little wooden platform. She looked at it.

"Too high, can you lift me up?" There was a little flirting going on then as well. She was getting used to and liked being picked up. Dave just said,

"Heck yeah." He loved picking her up. Good old mom was watching from the kitchen and smiled when Dave came in. He had noticed her looking and said innocently.

"You ever picked Tahlia up mom?" Mom,

"Just the feet; I'm guessing you have." He headed for the fridge.

"I carried her downstairs for breakfast when you were at work. She don't weigh nothing." Mom gave him a look, the arched eyebrow, and corrected him.

"Doesn't weight anything, hmm, and did you find carrying her rewarding?" Dave stopped; he knew something was cooking in mom mind. The next question confirmed it. "Where was she sleeping?"

"I said she could sleep in my bed." He could see both his mother's eyebrows go up slightly. Her son got it and jumped to his defence. "I wasn't in there with her!"

"I know son, but maybe we should have a little talk." Dave still didn't really seem to get it.

"About what?" She sighed, surprised he didn't catch her tone.

"Just go and get her."

"Ok." Dave headed out to find the other person of interest. When they entered the kitchen they noticed she was sitting with her head in her hands. She had been thinking, life was pretty complicated before this little girl landed in her house. The voice in her head; her husband deciding to go and sort some things out, whatever that meant. She was a ER nurse, so there were no quiet days or evenings there. And of course, she was a mother as well. David was a great kid, but, he was a thirteen year old boy and Mother Nature had been as they say, driving hard to the hoop. She looked up at them and smiled; she knew she was the parent; had to somehow always be the rock. She chose her opening word on purpose.

"Children." Dave smiled back; he was developing some ideas about the theme of this conversation.

"Mother, s'up?"

"What's the plan for sleeping tonight?" Dave was a smart kid and was now sure where his mother was heading, but also liked to mess with her.

"I figured she'd bunk with me." Tahlia swatted Dave lightly.

"Cheeky boy." This actually relieved Dave's mother

"So you know about all this?" Tahlia blushed, both smart, intuitive and informed.

"I do."

"I know you like David." She smiled.

"Of course I do, my dad got to know you and knew David would be a good host."

"Did your dad like that you transported here?"

"No, you probably know he's still upset." Dave's mom touched the little girl's hand.

"He keeps reminding me to look after you, so...in that vein. I don't think you can sleep in the same room as David."

Dave was staying out of this conversation; he knew of course, his mother was right. Truthfully, he was finding the whole business anything but easy, excluding the fact that in some very weird way sort of gave birth to her and watched her grow in his room. She was supposed to be like a sister, but, and that was a big but, he definitely did not have sister feelings about her. In spite of that got the feeling from his mom that somehow he was supposed to pretend she was. For Dave, that was a ship that was never built, never mind sailed. He'd never had a sister so really didn't know how you feel about one. He only knew about how Joey felt about his. He sure didn't think like that about Tahlia. One thing he knew, his feelings for her were not brother love, but the other one. Quite simply, no matter how bizarre she came into his life, he viewed her as his first girlfriend. There was nothing he could think of that was going to change that. How complicated in the long term it was going to be to have your first girlfriend live with him had not really occurred to Dave. This to date was the greatest thing to ever happen to him and he was not thinking about any issues. I bet you can think of a few yourself.

"Ok guys, I made the spare bedroom up and sweetheart, you can have it for your room. I left a few more clothes there and some girl stuff." She nodded, not really looking like that pleased her, but said,

"Thank you Mrs. Joseph." Dave's mother seemed pleased this issue was solved.

"Ok, I'm tired, hitting the hay, you guys?"

"I'm beat too mom." Tahlia smiled,

"Good night all." With that she headed upstairs she knew were the room was.

For Dave sleep was coming slowly. He was lying in the dark looking up at his ceiling; lots of thoughts swirling around in his head. At least the room had a skylight so he could see the late night sky, something to do. He was thinking, a zillion stars up there, and somehow I got my own alien from out there somewhere. He was hoping to see a meteor but when none appeared he turned on this side and noticed the pillow that she had used. The dent was still in it from where she slept. He leaned closer. Mother Nature was sitting in a nearby chair, smiled smugly, thinking, this game is easy.

"I wonder?" He took a sniff. "Whoa, sure enough, what is that smell?" It smelled like some kind of flower garden, actually made him a little dizzy. "What the heck is that? Smells nice but..," He fell back and looked at the ceiling getting his bearings again. He muttered to himself, a character trait of only children.

"Ok, I'll be fine."

Then the evening got even more adventurous. He sensed somebody in the room with him and heard a,

"Shh, it's me." Tahlia had pealed the covers back and crawled into his bed, looking at him. Poor Dave said in a loud whisper.

"What, what, what!"

"I'm lonely, it's like being in that metal cylinder." Dave just said,

"Ok, now…what?" To his relief she just said,

"I want to cuddle, lonely, that ok?" He spoke as quietly as he could, not wanting to wake up his mother for several reasons. Then he noticed,

"You're naked!" She shrugged.

"Yeah, who sleeps in clothes?" Dave was just holding it together.

"Ok, what am I supposed to do?" She smacked him lightly,

"Cuddle me, I'm cold and lonely."

"Ok, mom is going to be really ticked." She just shrugged and put her head on Dave's shoulder. She realised cuddling instructions were necessary.

"Ok your left arm can go around my shoulder." She actually grabbed it and put it in place. "Ok your right hand can go on my right shoulder." More instructions, "you can't play with my girls though." Dave almost let out another,

"What!" He of course did what he was told. She snuggled in place a little closer.

"There all tucked in." She whispered, "thank you." Then Dave got another burst of perfume. Another hoarse whisper.

"What is that?" She giggled quietly.

"Oh, our girls, have some kind of natural perfume. When we feel safe and loved around a boy it, just happens." Dave whispered.

"You think you're a little bit evil." She gave him a little smack.

"Just enough to be interesting." He gave her shoulder a little squeeze.

"You are interesting, and, you're safe with me." She nodded and leaned cleaner and gave him a gentle kiss on the cheek."

"I know." Poor Dave got another burst and would have fallen over if he was standing up. Just then, almost on cue arrived Joey. Joey the family cat not Joey his somewhat annoying but mildly lovable buddy. He'd been outside, up to no good when the air got a little too crispy for his majesty, so he came through the cat door looking for a warm bed. He usually slept with Dave as his mom wouldn't let him around at night. He landed with a soft thump on what was now their bed. They could hear him purring as he padded up the bed, tail hooked over, heading for warm bodies.

"Joey you flea bitten sack." More purring.

"What is that?" She had never seen a cat.

"That is Joey, a common house cat." He reached over and scratched his ears. "Completely useless, but what can you do." Tahlia made a big fuss.

"So he's a pet?" She took over rubbing his ears. "He's so soft and beautiful. Hi Joey, I'm Tahlia, you can cuddle with me anytime." Joey's got closer to her face, the purring got even louder, as he rubbed his head against her warm chin. He was in cat heaven, two warm bodies to cuddle with and a cool fall evening. Dave rubbed his ears as well.

"Yeah, he's a pet, can we go to sleep now?" She leaned over him.

"Yes, we can, I'm not lonely now." She took his face in her hands and gave him a gentle kiss, this time on the lips. It came with another burst of perfume; she let him go and put her head back on his shoulder. Poor, or not so poor Dave, depending on your attitude about adolescent romance took a moment to collect his thoughts. This had been his first kiss and it was, well, spectacular. Her lips were warmer than the rest of her body. Joey had dug down between the two of them; he would remain with them for the rest of the night.

Dave would start to drift off to sleep, after he had recovered. Finally all the bed mates, human, alien and feline drifted off into a gentle warm sleep. The whole world should be as lucky. Dave thought as he drifted off that his buddy Joey would love to hear about this evening. He decided, maybe a story left untold.

Come On David, You'll be Late for School

Well they do say all good things come to an end. Because of the late night festivities Dave had forgotten to set the alarm on his phone. And also because sleep was let's just say, somewhat interrupted the two of them were sound asleep when you know who stuck her head in the door.

Now children often forget their parents have lives beyond looking after them. This was one of those days for Dave's mom. She knew she had a couple of hours of overtime tacked onto her twelve hour shift at the hospital. Hospital administration seemed to think labour shortages are fixed with overtime for the current staff. Also she had to hang with a doctor she did not like from the first day she met him. At home on days like that all she wanted to do was make a large coffee and sip it on the way to work. Dave was old enough to get himself a bowl of cereal and get to the bus on time. Today was not starting well. She stuck her had in the door.

"Come on David, you're late; what the…!" She looked at what appeared to be adolescent bliss and put both her hands on the door frame and hung her head.

"Oh good! My son's in bed with a girl!" With that the three of them awoke with a start. Joey knew things were heading south and bolted for the door, his food dish and the cat door for a bathroom break. Dave looked at Tahlia and said,

"Oh, oh." Mother was standing with her hands on her hips.

"You two, cannot, and I mean cannot sleep together. For god's sake you're thirteen!" Tahlia came to first.

"My fault Mrs. Joseph, I was lonely. We didn't do anything." Dave's mom rolled her eyes.

"Ok, not this time." She had science fiction images of some kind of alien love child her thirteen year old son and wandering, whatever this girl was would produce. The jury was still out on that. She re-stated her feelings loudly.

"You two cannot sleep together, got it!" Tahlia started to sniff.

"Sorry Mrs. Joseph, my fault, Dave was really sweet." Another eye roll,

"I'm sure he was, you got clothes on under there?" She blushed,

"Well Dave has, I don't." Mother leaned back against the door frame.

"Of course, clothing optional. Ok Dave, get your butt out of there and get off to school. Tahlia, what's your plan, other than get some clothes on!" She sniffed again,

"I'll just hang here; sorry Mrs. Joseph." She stood for a second.

"Ok I'm off to work to support this…" She looked again at her now two children. "To support whatever this is!" With that she turned and left. The lady of the house was obviously ticked. Dave was out of the bed in a flash. The shower seemed like a good spot for now. Now Dave often used humour to try to lighten heavy moments. This was one of those times when it wasn't a good idea. He stopped on the way to the bathroom.

"You know we could make one of those sex-ed films today…be more fun that school." Mother was still not amused.

"I am going to smack you one day!" Dave had to unfortunately chuckle.

"Not funny?" Mother pointed to the shower.

"Not funny! Git!"

Starry Night

Joey came bounding down the path to the footbridge were he and Dave gathered after chores. He landed with his usual thump.

"You did all the chores." Dave nodded.

"Yep, needed something to do." Joey sat down next to him for a minute. He knew something was up.

"Thanks, what' going on?" Dave just shrugged,

"Nothin'." Dave lay back on the bridge and looked at the stars. Joey joined him and looked over. His buddy was obviously bugged about something.

"Come on, what's going on?" Long sigh,

"Tahlia's gone."

"Gone where?" Dave shrugged and pointed up at the sky.

"Up there somewhere I guess."

"Ok, how'd she get there?"

"Her cylinder's gone, she's gone." Joey was confused, then again he often was.

"So what'd she do shrink back down and go back up your butt?" You could even hear Dave laughing up at the house. Even though he couldn't remember feeling worse, his friend had a knack of making him laugh.

"No dopey; I would have noticed that. No I guess she just got in it and left somehow." Finally Joey had a good question.

"Why?" Dave had to make sure.

"You won't tell anyone?"

"No, what's going on."

"Well, mom thought me and Tahlia were getting friendly." Joey chuckled.

"Duh."

"Yeah, well we had separate rooms, but, she came into my room in the middle of the night and crawled into bed with me."

"What!" you could also hear that at the house. "What, did you?"

"No, but, she was naked." Another.

"What! Why?"

"She said she was lonely." Now Joey took a moment, and being an adolescent boy was developing his own pictures about this.

"So, what happened." Now is teenage boy world there really isn't a bigger story that that and Joey needed the details. Dave shrugged.

"Nothing, we cuddled and fell asleep. Mom found us in the morning." Joey knew that would not have gone well.

"Opps." Dave sighed,

"Opps for sure, mom was really ticked. Blew up at me and Tahlia, I went to school. When I came home she was gone." Joey was proud of himself for coming up with two good questions in the same sitting.

"Is she still inside your head?"

"Nope, I think she's gone for good." Joey commiserated with his best bud in the world.

"That sucks, she was so amazingly beautiful."

"Yeah, I know, more than that, really curious about everything, and so smart. She was trying to explain how they shrink everything to a photon. I don't even know what a photon is, kept nodding so she wouldn't think I'm stupid.

And so the two friends lay on the same bridge they had since they were old enough to wonder down near the water alone. Like all of us, they pondered the stuff they didn't understand and perhaps like the rest of us, never would. And Dave was full of new emotions, and at the bottom of it all, he just missed her and there was nothing he could do about it. Now adults would say,

"Come on, you're thirteen." Dave would say.

"Yeah, didn't like to see her cry and I miss her, so go chase yourself. There's nothing I can do but feel bad."

CNN

Well the next few days were pretty quiet around the Josephs. Mom and son were on good morning was a long conversation mode. Mother was intuitive enough to realise how hurt her son was and was wisely giving him the time and space to at least partially move on. At least she hoped he could move on. Finally after about a week she couldn't take it any more. They had been sitting opposite sides of the table eating cereal, the only sound being the scraping of spoons and chewing.

"David, I'm sorry she's gone; I was just worried." Dave figured it was time to bury the hatchet.

"I know; I didn't think she'd leave either. Didn't think she could. Talked to Gramps; he thought it was a one way ticket to Earth." His mother sighed; she was so pleased they were at least having a conversation. She was desperately choosing her words remembering a line from a T.V. series she liked.

"Be curious, not judgemental." She asked,

"I'm guessing there was something about her other than she was very beautiful?" The school bus horn went off. Mom was insistent,

"Forget the bus; I'll drive you later; or have a mental health day if you want." David smiled,

"I could use some mental health; it's quiet up here these days." He was remembering the kiss. "She seemed to give off some kind of aromatic drug, made me dizzy." Mother offered a suggestion.

"Maybe on her planet the girls choose and have some kind of high powered pheromone." Dave nodded remembering,

"She had something; whatever I just miss her, can't help it mom." She got up and came around behind him and gave him a long hug.

"Sorry I drove her away, really didn't think it would come to that. It all seemed so soon." Dave did agree.

"It was soon for me too, and you didn't know she would do that." His mom had a theory.

"I think she'll be back." Dave hadn't thought of that.

"Really?" She gave him another hug and a kiss on top of the head.

"Yes, she won't find a finer young man on any planet. Heck even your Gramps loves you; he don't like anybody. Take the day off, got to go to work."

Dave thought he'd whip himself up a Davewhich for breakfast, although he recalled it was the first breakfast he made for his departed love interest.

"Ok, got to move on. At least I can eat a Davewich again." Though he was occupied with cooking he got the feeling there was something going on out front. When he looked out the window; it looked like a circus was coming into the neighbourhood. Trucks and vans were pulling up outside his house, some with uplink satellite dishes. Dave figured it out quickly.

"Ok, they're looking for Tahlia, and for once was glad she wasn't here to deal with that. His mom's doctor 'friend' had shared the story, very likely for a good pile of cash, been done before. Dave also knew this would be the biggest story in the history of the planet. One thing Dave knew, he would not throw his girl under the bus, even if she wasn't there.

"Ok, go up, make her bed and stuff everything that was connected to her in a green garbage bag. Clothes she wore, girl stuff, everything." He could hear the knocking on the door, he was thinking, good thing my mom ain't here. There would be scratch marks on any newsman that got close.

With everything stowed away he answered the door. He was greeted by cameras and lights. He had decided before opening the door they were getting nothing. He had given his Grandfather his word on their family name, and had decided even if Tahlia was here he would protect her privacy and it would be her call to tell the world they were not alone. Considering the attention that was assembled it looked like they were looking for a circus act. A newsman stepped forward,

"Hello I'm Brad Cunningham from CNN, we have from reliable sources you have a very special girl here." Dave was determined to be cool.

"My mom's the only girl here and she's at work right now.

"That's not what our source said, he treated her." Dave stepped back,

"Take a look if you want, trust me, no girl." He thought about it but knew the publicity would not be good. A newsgroup invading a house of a minor child would not be well received these days. He just said,

"Maybe we'll just hang at the street for awhile." Dave smiled.

"If I were you I wouldn't be here when my mom comes home." He did seem mildly concerned.

"No?" Dave nodded.

"No, she's a momma lion. I just texted her that you all were here with pics. She's ticked." He winced, "could be ugly; I've seen her leave marks."

In that vein, momma lion burst through Doctor Roberts office door.

"I asked you to keep this in house! You're supposed to be a friend and colleague!"

"Cala, this is the biggest story in the history of mankind." Cala was so angry it was tough to organise a response.

"I don't care; they are both children, you know what kind of scrutiny she would be under. And there are people around who would kill her, afraid she might be importing some kind of alien virus." He went to speak; she held up her hand. "Shut up, the other thing is, one of them is my son." He just looked bewildered. "No, you wouldn't get it, not married, no children. David is my son." She got really close to him. "Nobody messes with my family!" She pulled back and took a breath. "And you better not spend the cheque yet, she's gone." He looked at her.

"Where?" Cala just turned and laughed,

"Right." She turned on the way out and gave him the pointy finger.

"Stay away from my family and me, never speak to me again!"

Three Years Later

Well time has a way of moving on. CNN went home the day after they came, realising there was no story. They never came back. Pretty tough to sell a story about a girl with no girl. The boys remained friends and wingmen through high school. Joey actually managed to round up a girlfriend. Dave did not even though he was told many times there are lots of fish in the sea. He to date had just not found a suitable substitute for Tahlia. He wondered if he would carry on until he was as old as his Gramps. Would he be shuffling around in his slippers, and grubby bathrobe, drinking too much whiskey and generally just being grouchy?

The boys would gather on the same bridge looking up at the same sky they had since they were children. One day Joey decided to raise the issue. This was big, as personal issues are seldom raised between male friends.

"You know you've been sort of moping for three years." Dave disagreed.

"Don't think so." Joey punched him.

"Yeah really, when you going to get over her?" Dave was distracted, still looking up trying to figure out what star she came from, no luck to date on that or the issue that Joey mentioned. He mused,

"Got to be from Andromeda, closest galaxy." He turned to his long time buddy.

"You're right, can't get her out of my head. Don't know how to do it." Joey was hoping for his long time friend.

"You think she'll come back?" Dave almost laughed.

"I do and I don't, actually, I haven't a clue." Joey reached over and gave him a light punch.

"Sorry man." With that the in depth discussion was over. They both knew there was really nothing either one of them could do. She was gone, and that was that.

One night he was sitting reading on the poor man's throne when he got a little twinge in his stomach.

"No way!" Then he heard, clink." When he looked, there it was, another one, about twelve centimetres long and about two centimetres wide. He knew without really knowing. He peered into the bowl, not the first place you look for a long lost girlfriend.

"Well hello darlin'" She at least did him the service of coming out before the gross stuff, but it was a careful retrieval and a disinfectant clean. He sat the cylinder on a clean towel and just sat and looked at it. He started talking to it immediately.

"You really in there? Why aren't you talking to me?" The first thing he did the next morning was measure it. Sure enough, it was a little longer. He knew from his Gramps this was not a communication antenna. Which he connected the dots and realised, that's why she wasn't talking to him. He wondered if the complete girl was in the cylinder and just got longer with time, or was she like some kind embryo. Very soon she was too big to fit on the night table and put her on a special mat on the floor. He of course was hoping it was her inside the cylinder, but really had no way to know for sure. Kind of like waiting for Christmas, but 2.0 plus.

Dave came down at breakfast and his mom was already at the cereal.

"Hey there darlin'." Dave just smiled and put the cylinder on the table on its towel.

"Mom, I think you were right; I think she coming back."

"She talking to you?" That was the only problem.

"No, your talker gone too?"

"Yep, nothing since she left. I got to say, that part is kind of nice." They both sat and looked at it. Dave had seen these cylinders before but still couldn't believe it.

"It's the most amazing thing, a whole girl in a photon, then it grows to this."

"I hope it's her dear, I really do, can't think on anyone else it would be." The old issues were long gone. Her son was older now, not a child. She came to understand how much he cared about this girl, and had come to admire it.

Dave got more excited as the days went by. The only fly in the ointment remaining was she was not talking to him like before. He didn't want to think it would be anyone or anything else but her. Every morning it was the same routine, check the cylinder as to how long it was and wait. What else could he do?

And finally, one day he woke up and noticed immediately the lid to the cylinder was off. Like before it somehow reminded suspended over it. Dave took a breath and rolled out of bed, tip toeing across the carpet as quietly was he could. He peered over the lid and there she was, the angel herself. Her eyes were still closed, hadn't woken up yet. He whispered,

"Tahlia." Her eyes fluttered open. She whispered sleepily.

"Hello David." He leaned a little closer.

"Well look at you." She gave him a sleepy smile.

"You can look at me." Dave would sure accommodate.

"Ok." She moved a bit.

"Well, how do I look?"

"Perfect, maybe a little taller?" She gave him a mischievous smile.

"Boobs a little bigger?" He shrugged,

"Hadn't noticed that." Another smile.

"Sure, whatever you say David, can you lift me out?" He very carefully lifted her out and put her in his bed and put some covers over her. That helped a bit.

"Get in with me, I need a cuddle, missed them." And so for the rest of the morning Dave was a human pillow and so glad of it. He hooked her hair behind her ear so her could look at her face as she rested from her long trip.

He heard a quiet knock at his door. Had to be mom.

"Hey David, can I come in?"

"Sure." She figured this was why he hadn't come down for breakfast. She tip toed over to the bed.

"Well there she is." David had to be sure.

"You ok with this?" His mother knelt down and moved some of her hair.

"My gosh she's beautiful." With that her eyes fluttered open.

"Hi Mrs. Joseph, you still mad at me?"

"Hey darlin', no bygones." Tahlia was very glad she was well received.

"You ok with this?" She leaned over and kissed the little girl on the forehead.

"You're part of this family now, for good?" She nodded.

"Can't get rid of me now."

"Good, very good, I'm going to work. David, you and Tahlia work all this out. She kissed her again,

"You know the big guy here's been moping for three years." She smiled.

"Good." David's mother got up.

"Ok, see you two at dinner." That gave Tahlia a thought.

"Yes I'll cook, you're son is wonderful, but a lousy cook."

"Hey I'm right here. What about the Davewich?" She giggled, starting to revive.

"It's edible, when you're hungry; which I am now!" Mrs. Joseph got up to leave as David was whining.

"You see what I'll have to put up with?" His mother smiled.

"Yes I do." She was thinking on the way out, a more bizarre family does not exist. But it's wonderful; she always wanted a daughter and now she had one. But this one was indeed special other than her son loved her as well. She was an,

An echo from the stars.

Dear reader,

Hope you enjoyed my short science fiction story. Not generally a science fiction writer, only two others in my list:

The Dark Side of the Moon and

Starfinder

These are a much longer read. Your call.

Got the idea from someone who deals in fibre optic cable data transfer. Got me to thinking if we could compress everything to a photon and fire it through space, we could move anything anywhere. I'm sure that would be difficult.

Your intrepid writer's summer writing office below, a long way from intergalactic travel.

Good sailing, Ron

100

Made in the USA
Middletown, DE
23 December 2021